Mighty Mighty MONSTERS

MONSTER MANSION

STONE ARCH BOOKS
a capstone imprint

created by Sean O'Reilly
illustrated by Arcana Studio

Mighty Mighty Monsters are published by Stone Arch Books, A Capstone Imprint
1710 Roe Crest Drive, North Mankato, Minnesota 56003 www.capstonepub.com

Library of Congress Cataloging-in-Publication Data
O'Reilly, Sean, 1974-
  Monster mansion / written by Sean O'Reilly ; illustrated by Arcana Studio.
    p. cm. -- (Mighty Mighty Monsters)
  Summary: The Mighty Mighty Monsters are convinced that they can spend the night
in a haunted mansion until they encounter the ghosts.
  ISBN 978-1-4342-2152-0 (library binding)
  ISBN 978-1-4342-3421-6 (paperback)
  1. Graphic novels. [1. Graphic novels. 2. Monsters--Fiction. 3. Ghosts--Fiction.] I.
Arcana Studio. II. Title.
  PZ7.7.O74Mon 2010
  741.5'973--dc22   2010004123)

Summary: When you're a Mighty Mighty Monster, spending the night in a haunted
mansion should be easy. Unfortunately, no one told that to the ghosts.

Printed in the United States of America in Stevens Point, Wisconsin.
072012
006876R

In a strange corner of the world known as Transylmania . . .

Legendary monsters were born

WELCOME TO TRANSYLMANIA

But long before their frightful fame, these classic creatures faced fears of their own.

o take on terrifying teachers and homework horrors, hey formed the most fearsome friendship on Earth . . .

Mighty Mighty MONSTERS

Vlad

Talbot

Witchita

Milton

Poto

Frankie

Igor

Mary

As a young wolfboy, one thing drove Talbot crazy . . .

HOOOOWL!

Well, besides a full moon.

HoOoOWL!

Hooooow will I ever finish my homework, Vlad?

CREEEEAKK

What was that noise?

There it is again!

CREEEEAKK

Uh-oh.

Pssst!

Over here, mateys!

Who is that?

Who cares! He's helping us!

Jump, Igor! The door is closing.

"During the fight, I headed toward shore to hide the treasure."

"Blackbeard and his men followed, but crashed on the rocky cliffs."

"Meanwhile, I hid the treasure inside the Monster Mansion."

"Since then, I have waited for my crew to return."

SPOOKY
FOREST

MONSTER
SCHOOL

FLAME OF
HALLOWEEN

CASTLE OF
DOOM

Mighty Mighty
MONSTERS
...BEFORE THEY WERE STARS!

IGOR

Nickname: Hunchie

Hometown: Transylmania

Favorite Color: Green

Favorite Animal: Camels

Mighty Mighty Powers: Super sixth sense; his "hunches" are never wrong; small enough to fit into tiny spaces.

BIOGRAPHY

Orphaned at birth, Igor often struggled to fit in at school . . . until he met the Mighty Mighty Monsters! These fearsome friends quickly adopted him into their creepy crew. And, although he remained shy, the young hunchback brought a special set of skills to the ghoulish gang. His "hunches" were never wrong, and he always steered the Mighty Mighty Monsters the right way. With a clear sense of direction, a keen intuition, and a unique style, it's no wonder he became a monster icon.

WHERE ARE THEY NOW?

Many people believe Igor first appeared in the 1931 movie *Frankenstein*. However, that hunchback was actually named "Fritz." The character "Ygor" did not appear until the movie *Son of Frankenstein* in 1938.

In the *Son of Frankenstein*, Bela Lugosi played the role of Ygor, Dr. Frankenstein's hunchbacked assistant. The actor had already gained fame playing Dracula in the 1931 movie.

Other famous hunchback characters include Quasimodo, featured in the 1831 novel *The Hunchback of Notre-Dame*. Disney made the story into a popular animated movie in 1996.

About Sean O'Reilly
and Arcana Studio

As a lifelong comics fan, Sean O'Reilly dreamed of becoming a comic book creator. In 2004, he realized that dream by creating Arcana Studio. In one short year, O'Reilly took his studio from a one-person operation in his basement to an award-winning comic book publisher with more than 150 graphic novels produced for Harper Collins, Simon & Schuster, Random House, Scholastic, and others.

Within a year, the company won many awards including the Shuster Award for Outstanding Publisher and the Moonbeam Award for top children's graphic novel. O'Reilly also won the Top 40 Under 40 award from the city of Vancouver and authored *The Clockwork Girl* for Top Graphic Novel at Book Expo America in 2009.

Currently, O'Reilly is one of the most prolific independent comic book writers in Canada. While showing no signs of slowing down in comics, he now writes screenplays and adapts his creations for the big screen.

GLOSSARY

calcium (KAL-see-uhm)—a soft, silver-white chemical element found in teeth and bones

dawn (DAWN)—the beginning of the day; sunrise.

hunch (HUHNCH)—an idea that is not backed by proof but comes from a feeling

manners (MAN-urz)—polite behavior

mansion (MAN-shuhn)—a very large and grand house

mate (MATE)—a friend

mood (MOOD)—the way a person is feeling

neighbor (NAY-bur)—someone who lives next door to you or near you

phantom zone (FAN-tom ZOHN)—an area where ghosts live

translate (TRANZ-late)—to express in a different language

tutor (TOO-tur)—a teacher who gives private lessons to one student at a time

vanish (VAN-ish)—to disappear suddenly

DISCUSSION QUESTIONS

1. Igor warned the other Mighty Mighty Monsters not to go inside the mansion. Should they have listened to him? Why or why not?

2. Skip was a ghost pirate. Why did the Mighty Mighty Monsters decide to help him?

3. All of the Mighty Mighty Monsters are different. Which character do you like the best? Why?

WRITING PROMPTS

1. The Mighty Mighty Monsters are based on classic movie monsters including Frankenstein, Dracula, and the Wolfman. Write your own story using one of these creepy characters.

2. Write your own Mighty Mighty Monsters adventure. What will the ghoulish gang do next? What villains will they face? You decide.

3. In this story, the Mighty Mighty Monsters helped out a new friend. Describe a time that you helped a friend or family member.

Mighty Mighty MONSTERS
ADVENTURES

The King of
Halloween Castle

New Monster
in School

Hide and Shriek

My Missing Monster

Lost in Spooky Forest